P9-CKJ-487

Aesop in California

To Rob Hansen

Christmas 2015
for Wyatt & Sierra
a book for story time
to examine & enjoy
from Angie Stein

AESOP IN CALIFORNIA

Doug Hansen

Heyday ♦ Berkeley, California

© 2013 by Doug Hansen

All rights reserved. No portion of this work may be reproduced or transmitted in any form or by any means, electronic or mechanical, including photocopying and recording, or by any information storage or retrieval system, without permission in writing from Heyday.

Library of Congress Cataloging-in-Publication Data

Hansen, Doug.
  Aesop in California / written and Illustrated by Doug Hansen.
      v. cm.
  ISBN 978-1-59714-235-9 (hardcover : alk. paper)
  1. Aesop's fables--Adaptations. 2. California--Pictorial works. [1. Fables. 2. Folklore. 3. California--Pictorial works.] I. Aesop. II. Title.
  PZ8.2.H253Aes 2013
  398.24'52--dc23
                              2012025265

Heyday is an independent, nonprofit publisher and unique cultural institution. We promote widespread awareness and celebration of California's many cultures, landscapes, and boundary-breaking ideas. Through our well-crafted books, public events, and innovative outreach programs we are building a vibrant community of readers, writers, and thinkers. To travel further into California, visit us at www.heydaybooks.com.

Printed in September 2013 in ShenZhen, Guangdong, China

Cover art by Doug Hansen
Book design by Lorraine Rath

Orders, inquiries, and correspondence should be addressed to:
      Heyday
      P.O. Box 9145, Berkeley, CA 94709
      (510) 549-3564, Fax (510) 549-1889
      www.heydaybooks.com

Manufactured by Regent Publishing Services, Hong Kong

10 9 8 7 6 5 4 3 2

Contents

Acknowledgments

I acknowledge the generations of artists and storytellers before me who crafted personal versions of these enduring fables. Their enchanting words and pictures endure in my memory and excite my creative impulses.

My insightful publisher, Malcom Margolin, suggested Aesop's fables as a subject for a new California-centric book and I leaped to say, "Yes, yes, yes please!" Aesop's fables promised a wonderland of opportunities for an artist and I am grateful that Heyday was confident enough in my abilities to turn me loose on such a glorious project.

Unexpectedly satisfying were the road trips to visit and photograph as many of the locales as possible. I suspected that no book or website could entirely provide the authentic details that would bring my illustrations to life—and I was right. Without the research trips, I would have missed visual details like the carpet of acorns in "The Oak and the Reeds," the knee-high field of wheat in "The Meadowlark and Her Children," and the high-rise kelp pile in "The Elephant Seal and the Kelp Fly."

Sister-in-law Debra Hansen was the enthusiastic chauffeur during a stormy weekend research safari through the Hollywood Hills and the Palos Verdes Peninsula. On another occasion, Debra, my wife, Susan, my brother Rob, and I endured a ludicrously protracted hike in Henry W. Coe State Park while we tried to reach the headwaters of Coyote Creek and maybe spot a green heron. Susan was the cameraperson on the expedition for "The Fox and the Grapes," photographing the fields and hills around Napa from our moving car.

Most memorable was a marathon three-day research trip with Rob—a noted biologist and birder. In early June we raced the oncoming summer heat to visit the scenic settings of four fables. We took a route that I venture to say is unique: Carrizo Plain to the Twentynine Palms oasis, around the Salton Sea, north to the Alabama Hills, then back home to Fresno. Rob drove, birded, and pointed out the subtle patterns and hidden wildlife all around us in those fantastic landscapes. Rob is my fraternal, indispensable nature expert and he is always graciously on call. This book is dedicated to him.

Herpetologist and nature photographer Bob Hansen (no, not a relation this time!) guided me to a conveniently accessible harvester ant mound. A photo of his Quail Lakes acreage covered in spring flowers inspired the panorama portrayed in "The Grasshopper and the Ants."

Where's a good blackberry bush when you need one? California State University, Fresno professor emerita of biology Ethelynda Harding told me just where to find one, at Kerckhoff Lake, and I took other reference photos for "The Prospectors and the Bear" around Auberry.

I have nothing but respect and affection for everyone at Heyday. Important aspects of this book came into being while the entire staff swapped ideas around a big conference table in 2010. I particularly want to praise the contributions of editor Jeannine Gendar, production director Diane Lee, and art director Lorraine Rath. Jeannine invariably cheers me and makes me feel that, yes, I can be a writer as well as an illustrator. Diane makes any plan seem possible and advocates tirelessly to ensure the integrity of my artwork. Lorraine has a refined graphic vision that embraces my work but takes the presentation beyond what I imagine. They all listen to my ideas and suggestions, reassure and encourage me, and without fail return my ideas to me in better condition than when I left them.

Welcome to the world of
Aesop in California!

Introduction

About Aesop and the Fables

Vivid stories of animals—and even trees—that talk and otherwise behave like humans have entertained adults and children since ancient times. No one knows for sure whether Aesop actually lived, but legend places him on the Mediterranean island of Samos about twenty-five hundred years ago. Aesop is described as an ugly, deformed field slave who nonetheless became famous for matching wits with his master, Xanthus the philosopher. Through clever use of his fables, Aesop gained freedom, wealth, and honor.

It's not known if Aesop ever wrote down his fables, or which fables are even his, but a collection in Greek exists from 300 BCE. The first English translation appeared in 1484. His legend has endured through the centuries and now hundreds upon hundreds of fables, from many sources, are ascribed to him. Idioms like "crying wolf," "sour grapes," and "the lion's share" reveal how the fables have become part of our everyday speech.

In early times it was up to the listener to interpret the meaning of each fable. Later, compilations offered ethical instruction by adding a "moral" at the end. Some morals now seem awkward and outdated, while others are perceived as timeless. I grew up hearing the fables with a moral attached and decided to present them in that familiar way.

Choosing the Fables, Animals, and Locations

After reading a dozen collections of fables I came to the happy insight that writers and artists throughout history have freely interpreted and pictured these universal tales in ways that reflected each creator's individuality and times. That realization inspired and encouraged me to retell and illustrate the fables my own way.

While illustrating my previous book, *Mother Goose in California*, it became clear to me that the wildlife and natural beauty of California offered many more illustrative opportunities than could fit in just that one book. As I had with the Mother Goose rhymes, I reimagined Aesop's fables as they would occur in California. I especially chose fables that offered opportunities to illustrate the gloriously diverse animals and habitats of the Golden State.

The animals of Aesop's long-ago Mediterranean world correspond comfortably with those found in California—for example, an African lion becomes a mountain lion, a nondescript tortoise a desert tortoise, and a lark a meadowlark. Sometimes a substitution enabled me to introduce more variety—a common crow is now a yellow-billed magpie, anonymous travelers become gold prospectors, and a bull is transformed into a bull elephant seal.

Modern perspectives reject the notion of noble lions, cunning foxes, and vain peacocks. Aren't those just human characteristics that we have assigned to unwitting beasts? These very fables have probably contributed to that practice. The behavior of real animals in the wild is endlessly absorbing and deserves to be treated authentically. Yet such characterizations are a storytelling device that is essential to the fables. Accordingly, I have integrated factual details of animal behavior into my stories while still adhering to the familiar form of each fable, in hopes that this combination will render the actions of these fabulous animals even more fascinating and memorable.

The Key to a Secret

Young readers and adults will enjoy the "Fabulous Facts" section at the back of the book. It offers abundant details about the animals, plants, and locations depicted in each fable.

Aesop has a secret to share with the most sharp-eyed readers. The first word of every fable begins with a big capital letter enclosed in a colorful rectangle. Do you see the animal climbing on or peeking from behind each letter? That same animal is hiding somewhere in the big illustration on the opposite page. Will you be the one to find them all?

—Doug Hansen

The Tortoise and the Hare

ackrabbit beat his feet on the sizzling, sandy desert like a drummer thumping a drum. *Thumpa-thumpa-thump!* The pounding drove Tortoise from his shady underground burrow. Tortoise blinked his little eyes. He saw the jumpy Jackrabbit and a crowd of desert animals gathered outside.

Jackrabbit stretched and showed off his muscles. "I am from the famous Hare family. Yesterday I raced and beat the lizard, the kangaroo rat, and the roadrunner." He grinned, showing his big front teeth. "I will beat you too, Tortoise. Your legs are stumpy and your shell is clunky. I challenge you to a race in the desert. When I race I always win, win, win!"

"Yes, my legs are short," replied Tortoise, "but they are just right for me. They are for digging, not for racing. But I will race you now. If I win, I will go back to my shady burrow and you must let me sleep in peace."

Jackrabbit laughed. The other animals laughed too. How could Tortoise ever beat Jackrabbit in a race?

Burrowing Owl took charge. "Attention! Start at the cholla cactus; go down the canyon and past the palm oasis. The first one to the creosote bush wins the race. Any questions? Ready? Get set. Go!"

Jackrabbit leaped from the starting line and showed off with some fancy *zig-zag-zigs* through the canyon. Tortoise had taken only one step. At the palm oasis, Jackrabbit paused. "That tortoise is as slow as a slug. He will take hours, and hours, and hours to get here. I can take a little nap in the shade and *still* win the race."

Tortoise was used to long walks. All alone, he passed through the canyon. He looked ahead at the oasis. There was Jackrabbit under a fan palm tree—asleep! Tortoise moved quietly by. He did not want to wake Jackrabbit and be teased about being stumpy and clunky.

Tortoise could see the finish line and a crowd of waiting animals. They cawed and yipped, whistled and hooted. He was nearly there. But then Tortoise heard a drumming sound. Jackrabbit was running after him at full speed!

Victory cheers had awakened Jackrabbit from his nap—but the cheers were not for him. Tortoise was almost to the creosote bush! "Why, why, why did I stop for that nap?" Jackrabbit gasped, as he raced to catch up. Jackrabbit stumbled, then bumbled, then tumbled across the finish line.

But he was too late. Tortoise had finished first and was strolling back to the peace of his shady burrow.

Slow but steady wins the race.

The Jay and the Peacock

jaybird explored a smooth, green lawn. The jay hopped and pecked in search of a snail or a bug, a berry or an acorn. Suddenly, Jay stopped his hopping. A long, fancy feather lay at his feet. It sparkled like a blue and green jewel, and at one end there was a spot like a golden eye. When Jay spied a second feather just like it, then another and another, he wondered if he was dreaming. Jay eagerly gathered them all up. "My feathers are blue and gray. What bird has feathers like this?"

His question was answered when several elegant birds walked into view. The birds trailed their long feathers on the lawn and perched among white stone pillars and cool fountains. Then Jay saw a sight he would never forget. One of the birds spread its blue and green tail feathers wide…then wider, like a jeweled fan with a hundred golden spots.

"So that is where these feathers came from," thought Jay. "Those must be peacocks! Oh, if only I could be so beautiful. What a fine life they lead among the pools and shady walkways, while I must scramble in the scrub with the common birds."

A bit of string on the lawn caught his eye and Jay had an idea. He tied the long peacock feathers to his own little tail of blue. Holding more peacock feathers under each wing, Jay was so sure he looked just like a beautiful peacock that he strolled up the lawn and joined the birds on the hill. "This is where I really belong," thought Jay, and he laughed with a sound like "Jree, jree, jree."

But the proud peacocks were not fooled by Jay's disguise. They rushed at Jay and pecked him from all sides. They pulled off the borrowed feathers and screeched, "You can't trick us! Get off this hill, you plain old thing, and go back to the scrub-jays." Jay hopped glumly down the hill, his wings dragging and his head drooping low.

The other jays had watched him the whole time and they did not welcome him back. "Don't look for pity from us. We saw you acting like a vain peacock with those feathers. You thought you were so good-looking. Well, you don't look so handsome now!"

It is not only fine feathers that make fine birds.

The Fox and the Grapes

A hungry fox jogged wearily past hills colored green, gold, and brown. Fox had traveled far from his den. He was thin and his coat was dull. Fox had found nothing in the fields to eat. He had caught no rabbits, mice, or birds, and even the grasshoppers flew out of his reach.

Night was the best time to hunt, but now Fox hunted in the heat of the day. He imagined the taste of cherries…or maybe berries…when suddenly he found himself walking in a shady place. Springy, green grass was cool under his paws. Fox looked around. He was in a tunnel of neatly painted white wooden posts. Twisting vines wrapped like ropes around the posts and climbed up to make a leafy green roof. But Fox wasn't interested in leaves.

Fox looked up. Grapes! Green and red and purple grapes glowed in the sun. Clusters were hanging from the roof of the arbor. Fox had tasted wild grapes before, but these were not wild; people had planted them. They were sure to be the sweetest and tastiest of all! The people had trained the vines to grow way up high on the white wooden trellis. It seemed like those people wanted all the best grapes, but Fox would get them somehow!

Fox leaped high, imagining the taste of the juicy grapes, but his jaws snapped shut on empty air. He tried a running start and jumped like a kangaroo rat. Poor Fox ended up in a tangle of scratchy weeds and stinging nettles. If only he could find a way to reach those grapes! It was not dignified, but Fox tried climbing the vines. Vine bark shredded and peeled under his scrabbling claws. A little bluebird flitting high among the grapes laughed as the frazzled fox tumbled to the ground again and again.

Fox was worn out from climbing and jumping. He was angry and embarrassed that the bluebird had seen his clumsy leaps. Fox brushed the stickers and dirt from his coat and smoothed his tail. As he walked away from the arbor he called over his shoulder so the bluebird could hear: "Don't waste your time on those grapes. I'm sure they're all sour anyway."

It's easy to find fault with what you cannot have.

The Grasshopper and the Ants

Once there was a grasshopper that was pleased by everything he saw. When Grasshopper looked at the spring and summer grasses around him, he saw a juicy, green meal. When he looked at tangled weeds, he saw his playground. And when he looked at the wildflowers, he saw a pretty place to perch and make his scratchy leg music. If you asked Grasshopper how to make leg music, he'd say, "Just rub your hind leg on your hind wing to make a *chrr-chrr-chrr* sound. It's easy if you are a grasshopper."

Grasshopper enjoyed watching the ants working busily on the ground below. From his perch he joked with the ants. "Why do you ants work so hard? There is food all around! I know how to enjoy life—just do what I do! Relax and chew, make some music, and look at the view."

Some of the ants were carrying seeds and bits of leaves to their underground storerooms. They said, "Yes, there is food all around, but it makes sense to save plenty for later." Other ants brought sand and pebbles out of the burrow and kept the ant-mound tidy. They said, "We like our work! Look what a big mound we have made; and our tunnels go far and deep."

One day the sky turned gray and the earth grew cold. There were no more flowers or green grass for Grasshopper. The chilly wind scattered the dead leaves left over from summer. Most of the ants were busy inside their mound, but one ant stayed outside on lookout duty. Her job was to warn the other ants if she found any horned lizards nearby. Instead, the scout found Grasshopper hungry and stiff with cold. "Please give me something to eat. I think I'm starving," begged Grasshopper. "Why should we share with you?" said the scout, "You played all summer while we worked! Can you name just one thing that you did for us?"

Grasshopper whispered weakly, "What about my leg music? Surely my scratchy music made your work just a teeny bit easier?" The ants agreed that Grasshopper was the only insect around who made music for them. So they decided to share a teeny bit of their food with the musical Grasshopper, and he promised that next year he would work first and play later.

Prepare today for the needs of tomorrow.

The Magpie and the Basket Bottle

A magpie hunted and pecked at the dry Central Valley dirt. Magpie was used to foraging for grasshoppers or acorns, but today she needed water. A plain of dry grass blazed yellow in the summer sun, but there was not a tree or bush in sight to signal water. "I must find water or I will die," thought Magpie, "and then all my magpie friends will be sad."

Magpie met an antelope squirrel and asked, "Squirrel, where can I find water?" Squirrel said, "Try the Rock," then dashed back down her burrow. Magpie went on. "Oh! Here is a lizard. Maybe he knows which rocks have water." Lizard only hissed, "Find the Painted Rock!" and disappeared into the grass.

There was a clump of dark rocks in the distance. As Magpie got closer, her sharp eyes saw marks, patterns, and pictures there. The Painted Rock! Magpie knew that people must have painted those designs, and Magpie hoped that people had left behind some water, too. Magpie thought she could smell water, but where? In the shade of the rock Magpie found a tightly twined basket. It was shaped like a bottle…with a little bit of water, way down in the bottom! "Water! At last," she rasped.

Magpie rushed to dip her beak into the water…but her beak was too short to reach it. If she tipped the bottle over, all of the precious water would spill in the dirt. How could she get it? Magpie tilted her head this way and that as she thought about a way to get to the water. Clever Magpie found a little stone and dropped it, *plunk*, into the bottle. The water rose a bit higher in the basket bottle! With her sharp eyes she found more pebbles and little things people had left behind. Magpie dropped each small object in the bottle—*plunk, plunk, plunk;* and each time, the water rose higher.

Finally the precious water was near the top of the basket bottle. Magpie poked her yellow bill in and drank and drank. She had never tasted anything so refreshing! Magpie would never forget the trick she had learned.

Necessity is the mother of invention.

The Elephant Seal and the Kelp Fly

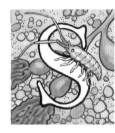 eventy female elephant seals dozed in the sand on a sunny California beach. The female seals were called "cows" but didn't look like the cows that live on land. These seal cows were smooth and golden gray, had big dark eyes, and weighed a ton. They cuddled close to each other, each one with a look on her face that was very much like a contented smile. "I know there are seventy because I counted them all," squeaked a busy little insect called Kelp Fly.

Kelp Fly had a good view of everything that went on at this beach because she was clinging to the highest place around, the huge, droopy nose of a bull elephant seal! Bull was not pretty, but he *was* pretty big. Bull was bigger than all the cows and tougher than all the other male elephant seals. He weighed five thousand pounds—as much as a car. Bull could make amazing roars, snorts, and grunts through that great big nose. Sometimes Kelp Fly was nearly blasted from her perch. "Yes, it sure can be noisy up here, but what a view," she announced.

"No storms in sight today," reported Kelp Fly in her tiny voice. "It looks like the other male seals have finally learned to stay away from us," she told Bull. "And the seventy cows look sleepy and safe." Kelp Fly wasn't sure if Bull was listening, so she crept down to the tip of Bull's big nose and waved two of her little red legs for attention. "Attention, Bull! It looks like we have everything running smoothly here. If you need me I'll be down at the kelp pile."

Bull blinked in surprise, blew out a big snort, and rumbled, "Hmmm? What did you say your name is? Kelp Pile? You say you are leaving? Well, go right ahead. I never noticed you before anyway, so I guess I won't miss you when you are gone."

"Well then, I'll just leave right now," sniffed the tiny Kelp Fly angrily. "But you'll never find another fly like me!" And she darted away to the kelp pile.

Sometimes we think we are more important than we really are.

King Log and King Stork

bunch of noisy bullfrogs lived in a pond near a salty inland sea. The biggest bullfrog puffed out his chest and spoke to the others. "Brrr-um. Fellow frogs, we have water to swim in and food to eat, just like the frogs in all the other ponds. But what if we had a king? No other frogs have a king. A great king would make us better than the rest." So all the frogs called to the heavens and begged for a king.

Suddenly a big log fell into the pond. *Ka-splash!* Frogs leaped and hid in the bushes or ducked underwater. After a while, the frogs peeked from their hiding places. They saw that they were in no danger. In fact, their king was a log.

"Welcome King Log, ruler of the frogs." They cheered and they danced and they swam around the log, but King Log said nothing, because logs are only wood. Before long, the king no longer seemed so special. The baby frogs took naps on King Log. Frisky young frogs bounced on King Log. But King Log, being made of wood, only floated and bobbed in the water.

"What kind of king is this?" croaked the grown-up frogs, "This is not a great king. This king is worthless. Let's ask the heavens to send us *another* king."

So a new king, King Stork, flapped down from the heavens and stood in the middle of the pond. The frogs were suddenly quiet when they saw King Stork.

Glomp! King Stork snatched up the biggest bullfrog for breakfast. Then he swallowed another for lunch and one for a snack. King Stork's deadly bill speared and snared one frog after another. "Someone save us from this king!" wailed the frogs, "Or he will eat the rest of us for dessert!"

The foolish frogs got just what they had asked for. They wanted a new king and now they had one.

Be careful what you wish for.

The Meadowlark and Her Children

other Meadowlark and her three children lived in a waving, whispering field of golden wheat. They lived in a little hidden nest with a roof of grass and, in front, a path like a tunnel where the three meadowlark children could play. Mother Meadowlark was the clever weaver who made the roof of their little nest and it was she who taught her three fledgling children to understand the language of humans.

Her littlest fledgling flitted to the nest one day, cheeping with excitement.

"Mother, I heard the man say the wheat is tall and ripe. The man said that his friends promised to help him with the harvest. What does 'harvest' mean?"

"'Harvest' means that the man will bring a harvester machine of wheels and smoke and iron to cut down the wheat. Blades on the machine will cut and thresh the wheat, and the wheels will crush everything in the field. When the harvest comes we must leave our cozy nest and fly away. But you can sleep easy tonight, because it is not harvest time yet."

Next day, the middle-sized fledgling fluttered to the nest. "Mother, the man said he will start the harvest as soon as his friends come to help. Is it time to fly away now?"

"Don't worry," said Mother Meadowlark. "He will wait and wait, but his lazy friends will not come. You can sleep easy tonight."

Next morning, the biggest fledgling flapped back to the nest. "Mother! I heard the man say he is tired of waiting for help from his friends. He is sitting in the seat of the harvester machine. He is wearing his straw hat and work shirt. Is it time to fly away now?"

"Yes," said Mother Meadowlark, "he is ready to do his own harvest work. We must all fly away now!" Together the meadowlarks flew fast and low, away from the smoke of the harvester. That night they would all sleep easy in a new nest.

Your mother knows best.

The Lion and the Mouse

ne evening a little deer mouse scurried and scampered through the brush. Mouse liked seeds and packed as many into his cheek pouches as he could hold. Mouse saw some funny-looking boulders nearby. He decided to explore the piles of big, egg-shaped rocks.

Exploring can be risky, and the careless mouse bumped right into the nose of a mountain lion! Lion snatched Mouse up in one big paw. Sharp claws pinched Mouse, and the lion's yellow eyes were scary and bright. Mouse swallowed the seeds. "Oh please, don't eat me. I'm a deer mouse, not a deer!"

Lion smiled and growled, "It's true I like deer—in fact, I just finished eating one. But you can be my dessert."

Mouse spoke bravely to Lion. "Can't I be your friend instead of a snack? You never know when you might need my help."

Lion roared with laughter at this idea. "*Raar har har!* Mister Mouse, how funny you are! I am the strongest and biggest animal around. Everyone fears my claws and teeth. How could you ever help me? Why, I'm embarrassed to be seen with you! Run away now. *Ha ha ha-raw!*" So Mouse ran into the dark, glad to escape the mountain lion.

Days later, Mouse heard a familiar growling near his burrow. "*Graar. Raar!*" "Oh! That sounds like Lion," thought Mouse, "but he is not laughing." Mouse crept carefully toward the noise and saw a terrible sight. Lion was trapped in a cage of metal and wire and could not even turn around. Now Lion's yellow eyes were afraid and shone with tears. "Hunters tricked me into this trap and I cannot get out! I am strong, but not stronger than iron."

Mouse had seen a mousetrap before and he looked closely at the lion trap. As he squeezed through the wire to help Lion, Mouse said, "You see? Sometimes it's good to be small." Mouse found the cord to open the trap. He grasped it in his tiny mouth and tugged it close to Lion's big paw. "Lion, now is the time to use your strength. Pull on this cord, and then you can back out of the cage. See, the trap is open!"

Swiftly, Lion scrambled from the cage and turned to thank the clever mouse. "Mouse, you rescued me from the hunter's trap. From now on, you and I are the best of friends!"

Even the mighty may need the help of the small.

The Roosters and the Eagle

wo roosters lived in a pretty little barnyard, with the blue sky above and the warm earth below. There were dozens of hens in the henhouse, and just the right amount of corn and grain to eat. Some hens admired the rooster with the golden wings, and other hens were fans of the rooster with the white wings.

The two proud roosters could never get along. Gold Wing thought he should be top rooster and get to stand on the roof of the henhouse. White Wing insisted that he was top rooster and the henhouse roof belonged to him. Only one of them could be top rooster, so they agreed to have a showdown. "We'll decide this with a barnyard fight…rooster style!" When the hens heard that, they ran up the ramp to the henhouse for safety. They did not like to see the roosters fight.

Gold Wing and White Wing came beak to beak in the silent barnyard. The two birds circled; they each lowered a wing. Neck feathers flared and both roosters seemed to grow in size. *Screeech!* The two roosters dashed to the attack but no one could tell who struck first. There was pecking and gouging. Sharp claws scrabbled and rooster spurs cut as the birds exchanged kicks in midair. Gold feathers and white feathers fell everywhere.

In a minute it was quiet again. A hen peeked from the henhouse and saw Gold Wing lying on his back in the dust. White Wing strutted around and crowed in victory. "Cock-a-doodle-doo! I am the top rooster!" White Wing flapped to his perch on the henhouse roof, puffed out his chest, and proudly declared, "I am the boss of the barnyard!"

Then White Wing looked out over the pretty little farm. He crowed, "*And* I am the lord of the farm!" But that still wasn't enough for him. Soon, White Wing cocked his head and gazed at the distant mountains. "All birds in the world should bow to me too," he announced. "I am the champion bird of all time!"

Just as White Wing gave another "cock-a-doodle-doo!" a great golden eagle dropped from the sky like a lightning bolt. In a storm of white feathers, the eagle grabbed the rooster by the neck. The eagle laughed as he flew away with his prey. "Silly, vain rooster. Looks like I'm the champion this time."

Pride goes before a fall.

The Oak and the Reeds

When the west wind began to blow, every reed and tree along the river was touched by the breeze. Cattails nodded their fuzzy brown heads. Bulrushes leaned this way and that and rattled their reedy stems. The oak tree fluttered its leaves and a few floated to the ground. Some acorns fell too, going *plop, plop.* Jays and ground squirrels quickly scurried after the nuts.

The bulrushes looked up at some dark clouds and said, "Get ready for a storm." The cattails shivered, "Yes, yes, a big storm is coming." Oak Tree flexed his sturdy branches and curled his bark in a smile. "I have seen many seasons and a hundred storms. I am the biggest and oldest thing on the river, and storms don't bother me."

The west wind blew harder. Rain clouds hung in the sky like a dark, ragged blanket. Oak leaves and raindrops scattered everywhere. The jays flew fast, away from the storm. A ground squirrel shut her eyes and dived into a burrow. The cattails and bulrushes bent far, far over. They said, "If we bow to the west wind, we will be safe." But Oak Tree gripped the earth with many roots and held its branches high. Oak Tree shouted above the storm, "I am great and strong. My trunk is thick, my branches long. I will not bow to any wind!"

But then a blast from the west wind hit Oak Tree like an invisible axe. Oak Tree toppled over. His branches thrashed and waved, but the soft ground could not hold him up. *Crash! Splash!* The mighty Oak Tree fell down and rolled helplessly in the river as his bare roots scratched vainly at the sky.

The bulrushes and cattails bent low and stayed down until the storm was over. "Poor Oak Tree," they said. "We survived and he did not. We know better than to stand up to the west wind."

It is better to bend than to break.

The Little Crab and His Grandmother

ittle Crab liked to play on the rocks at the sandy, splashy, salty seashore. Grandmother Crab crouched in the seaweed and watched him. She kept a sharp eye on Little Crab. "Grandmother, watch me run!" He scampered to the left and he scampered to the right.

"That is no way for a crab to walk," said the grandmother sternly. "Look straight ahead and walk forward."

"Yes, Grandmother," said Little Crab. He was always a good crab and wanted to please his grandmother. Little Crab looked straight ahead, but when he tried to walk to the front, he went sideways instead.

"You know better than to walk like that," snapped Grandmother. "It seems that every animal in the tide pool knows how to move properly except you! The sea slug swims along in a graceful ripple. Starfish creep smoothly along on a thousand tiny tube feet. And the limpet…well, the limpet is smart enough to just sit still. Now mind me, Little Crab, and do as I say," snipped Grandmother.

Poor Little Crab. He tried again, but his five pairs of legs would only take him sideways.

Grandmother Crab was so mad she looked even crabbier than usual. She waved her claws in the air and said, "I'll show you how it's done." Then she got up on her pointy toes and said, "This is how a crab is supposed to walk."

Grandmother Crab took one step, and then…and then…she went…sideways! Little Crab had good manners, so he did not laugh or say one word to Grandmother. Grandmother tried to keep her dignity and sputtered, "Well, I suppose we crabs may choose to go sideways if we want." And so they did.

Practice what you preach.

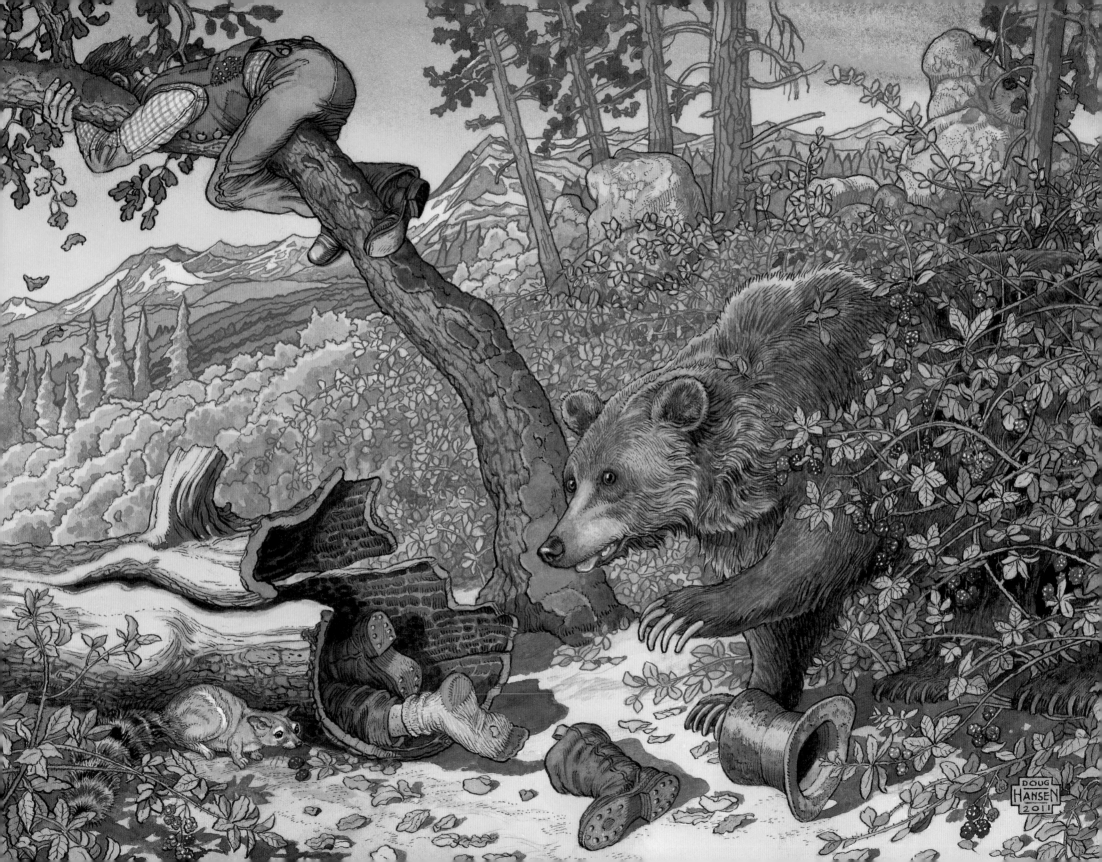

The Prospectors and the Bear

wo tired prospectors dropped their work tools on the ground. *Clunk!* Late afternoon in the rocky, rugged gold country was the time to return to camp. Soon the mountain valley would be in shadow. One man wore a tall top hat. "I hope tomorrow is the day we find gold," said Top Hat. The other man had a red vest with many patches. "We'll just stick together until we get rich," said Red Vest, "That's what friends do."

The two men had not been in the wild country for very long. So when their path led them into a blackberry thicket, they stopped to pick some. They didn't know that grizzly bears like blackberries too.

Sure enough, a grizzly bear rose from the blackberry patch and made a startled noise. "Wouf." Berry juice dripped from his long claws and from his fearsome jaws. Up on his hind legs, Grizzly was taller than the tip of the top hat!

Both frightened men yelled, "Climb a tree!" But there was only one tree nearby. Red Vest got up the tree first.

"Help me get in the tree with you!" cried Top Hat.

"Sorry, friend," said Red Vest, "there's only room for me."

With no other place to hide, Top Hat squirmed into a hollow log. He lost one boot and his hat!

Grizzly sniffed the log. He sniffed Top Hat's feet. The feet did not smell sweet! The bear tried the other end of the log. "It's all over for me," thought Top Hat. "He is going to bite off my head!"

Grizzly put his huge muzzle close to the man's ear—and whispered! Then the bear disappeared into the forest to search for a less crowded berry patch.

Top Hat crawled out of the log. He was surprised to still have a head. He pulled on his boot and he put on his crushed hat. He was angry because Red Vest hadn't shared the tree. Red Vest climbed down from the tree. He felt ashamed…but also curious. "It sure looked like that grizzly was whispering in your ear. But bears can't talk."

"Well, *that* bear could talk," Top Hat replied, "and he told me to find a new friend!"

Adversity is the truest test of friendship.

The Heron and the Fish

ne misty morning, a hungry heron strode into a stream in search of her daily fish breakfast. Her bill was like a sharp spear pointed at the water. Her yellow eye peered through the ripples and reflections in the stream, waiting for the slightest movement that would show where to find a delicious fish.

There! A crayfish foolishly crept along the gravelly streambed, right where Heron could see it. But Heron did not snap up the crayfish. "Pshhh," croaked Heron, "what a waste of time. I want something better than that. A crayfish won't even make one bite for me."

After a while, a little stickleback flashed into view. Heron thought, "Huh! That fish has too many little bones for me to fuss with. I'll just wait for a bigger fish."

It took a while, but Heron saw a perch hiding in the shadow of the stream bank. "I don't think so!" said Heron. "A perch is a dull meal for the likes of a fine bird like me. What I'd really like is a nice juicy trout." The lucky perch swam quickly away before Heron could change her mind.

The sun was rising higher; it was past Heron's breakfast time. Heron practiced holding very still, and waited, and waited some more. By noon, the harsh sun was blazing down on Heron. No fish were in sight. No tasty trout showed up to be speared by Heron's deadly bill. Heron was hungrier than ever.

Heron stood in the little stream all day and did not catch one fish. She thought about all the fish she had seen that morning. "I guess a bony old stickleback isn't really so bad…and a perky little perch would feel good sliding down my throat. I'd even take a crunchy little crayfish. Why didn't I just eat them when I had the chance?"

At sunset, Heron flapped wearily to her nest, high in a solitary tree. She could barely fall asleep, she was so grumpy and hungry. After fishing all day, the hard-to-please hunter with the deadly bill had eaten only one slimy little snail.

She who is too picky may go hungry.

The City Mouse and the Country Mouse

ity Mouse went to visit his friend Country Mouse. The two mice did not see each other often, and City Mouse wanted to see the country. He huffed and scurried and puffed and hurried up a steep hill. He pushed through scratchy bushes and arrived at Country Mouse's burrow all dusty and hot.

"Welcome, City Mouse! It's a warm day; would you like a drink?"

City Mouse answered that he would like a fizzy soda or some chocolate milk. "Oh, I don't have those things here in the country, but I have some water."

City Mouse glumly sipped the water and looked at the burrow where his friend lived. Roots and stones were the only furniture.

"I hope you are hungry," said Country Mouse. "I saved a beetle for our lunchtime nibble."

City Mouse gulped because he did not like the taste of insects. He said, "Um, maybe we can eat later. Can we listen to some music instead?"

Country Mouse told him he did not have a radio or anything to play music on. It was very quiet in the country.

The sun began to set and city lights sparkled in the valley below. Now City Mouse wanted to get back to his city house. "Come home with me and have dinner," he said to Country Mouse. "I will show you why city life is the best!"

Off they ran, down the hill to the city. The two mice crossed many busy streets. *Honk! Honk!* "What is that awful noise?" asked Country Mouse.

"That's just a car horn!" said City Mouse. "Now hurry up these steps. This house is where I live! But be careful, there is a mousetrap by the wall." Country Mouse did not like the look of the trap or the strange, dark kitchen.

The humans had left a mess after a birthday party. Chips, pizza, punch, and cake were scattered everywhere. "Let's have a party too," whispered City Mouse. "This is the city life!" The two mice climbed eagerly to the countertop. But when the first pretzel went *crunch*, a black cat with yellow eyes jumped from the shadows. "Run!" squeaked City Mouse. But Country Mouse was *already* running; down the steps, across the roads, and back up the hill he went.

"I wonder how City Mouse can ever live in a horrible place like that? I'd rather stay in my quiet country burrow…and nibble on a beetle."

Better to snack in safety than to feast in fear.

Fabulous Facts

Aesop has more to share about the California animals, plants, and places in these fables.

The Tortoise and the Hare

When people think of California, a palm tree is usually part of the picture, yet the desert fan palms are the *only* palm trees native to California. Geologic faults, such as the famous San Andreas Fault (which extends all the way from Humboldt County to the Mexican border), allow precious water to seep to the surface in parts of the Mojave Desert, and palm trees grow there in shaggy-looking clusters. Dry palm fronds cover the tree trunks because people have never trimmed them. These palm oases are a refuge for migrating birds and some scarce desert creatures.

Desert Tortoise and Black-tailed Jackrabbit are racing at the Twentynine Palms oasis in Joshua Tree National Park. As Jackrabbit says in the fable, he is a member of the hare family. He has cleared a "scrape" on the ground to take his nap in. In contrast, the burrow of the desert tortoise may be as deep as ten feet underground.

A hooded oriole makes sure Jackrabbit is asleep, and a kangaroo rat, roadrunner, and burrowing owl wait at the finish line.

Look for the Coachella Valley fringe-toed lizard. The edges of the toes have a zigzag fringe—but if you try to get a close look, the lizard will zip away. A biologist friend of Aesop jokes that it is a "French toast lizard."

The Jay and the Peacock

In earlier times, wealthy people often owned peacocks because of the birds' exotic beauty. Around 1916 banker Frank A. Vanderlip Sr. brought peacocks to his estate in Rancho Palos Verdes, a peninsula community perched above the Pacific Ocean. Colonies of peacocks still roost there in the trees and roam the lawns. Pictures of the Vanderlip estate inspired the elaborate garden in the fable's illustration.

The showy and colorful bird we call a peacock is an Indian blue peafowl. The female is called a peahen, the babies are peachicks, and the fancy bird from the story is the male—a peacock. If you ever heard a peacock call, you would remember it! It's a startling scream—*pia-ow*.

Aesop thinks the western scrub-jay is also a handsome bird, with its bright black eye, feathers of blue, gray, and white, and a gray-brown "cape" on its shoulders.

Find the red admiral butterfly near some flowers.

The Fox and the Grapes

Grapes are grown in many parts of California, but the Napa Valley is notable for wine grapes. All different sorts of grapes are growing on this arbor.

The frustrated red fox has landed in the weeds and thistles. Burrs are stuck to his red fur. Red foxes are not native to the California lowlands—the gray fox, kit fox, and Sierra Nevada red fox are the native California foxes.

A pretty western bluebird is spying on the fox from the arbor. Grape growers like the bluebirds because they feed on insect pests.

The Grasshopper and the Ants

The grasshopper in the fable is a pallid-winged grasshopper. "Pallid-winged" means that its wings are very pale, but the dark markings on wings, legs, and body make excellent camouflage. Not only can grasshoppers fly, they can make sounds too. In the fable, lazy Grasshopper brags about the "leg music" that he makes by rubbing his raspy hind legs against his back wings.

Grasshopper likes to watch the ants at work. Have you ever watched the busy ants? Inside the tunnels and chambers of the ant-mound, some ants tend the queen, and others work in the nurseries. On the surface, individual California harvester ants wander far from the nest to search for seeds and then carry them back to the mound. The mounds are broad and circular, and the ants keep them clear of plants and debris. But some seeds still get dropped and in spring, a wall of wildflowers will encircle the mound. Grasshopper is chewing on a California milkmaids leaf. Behind him are curling, yellow-orange common fiddlenecks, and across the way are scarlet monkeyflowers. Closer to the ground are baby blue eyes and white popcornflowers.

Even though these ants can bite *and* sting, they have a dangerous enemy, the horned lizard—and a scout ant is watching out for them in the fable. Some people call this creature a "horny toad." The lizard might look like a big, scary dragon to the ants. Where is that lizard hiding?

The Magpie and the Basket Bottle

Aesop chose the lonely Carrizo Plain for his retelling of "The Crow and the Pitcher." Painted Rock is a dramatic, natural, sandstone amphitheater—a ceremonial site of the native Chumash people, who journeyed there from the California coast. Visitors to the Carrizo Plain National Monument can see red, black, and white pictographs like those on the walls behind Magpie.

Black-billed magpies are found all over the West, but the yellow-billed magpie is found *only* in central California. Clever Magpie is dropping pebbles into the basket bottle. Magpie might want to use the Chumash shell beads, skirt weights, and arrow straightener lying nearby. But how can a basket hold water? The Chumash people used hot stones to melt powdered tar inside their twined water baskets—that made them waterproof. Lucky for Magpie!

The antelope squirrel and blunt-nosed leopard lizard live on the Carrizo Plain. The lizard has good camouflage—can you find it?

The Elephant Seal and the Kelp Fly

Aesop visited Año Nuevo State Park to see the northern elephant seals. Adult male elephant seals have big droopy noses that amplify their roaring, grunting, and bellowing. Bull looks a little sleepy, possibly because he just arrived at the beach after swimming thousands of miles, or perhaps from diving a thousand feet deep. He also might be tired from fighting the other males. His chest is "cornified" with tough skin, like a callus.

After a mother seal has gone back to the ocean, her fat youngsters—called "weaners"—must finally take their first sea trip to find food. Until then, they lie around in sleepy bunches called "weaner pods."

Kelp Fly's scientific name is *rufitibia*—that means "red leg." Look in the kelp pile to find the funny-looking California beach hopper. Some people call it a sand flea.

King Log and King Stork

In California, the place to see the only stork in North America is down by the Salton Sea. This "sea" is fairly new. In 1905 an irrigation canal broke and for two years the Colorado River flooded into a desert basin, forming a new lake that was 195 feet deep! Now it is only 50 feet deep, and with nowhere to drain it gets saltier every year.

The Sonny Bono Salton Sea National Wildlife Refuge inspired the setting for the pond in this fable. The Salton Sea sparkles in the distance. Wood storks build their stick nests in the nearby cottonwood trees, and in fact, King Log came from a cottonwood tree. The distinctive rock formation behind the trees is Obsidian Butte.

Settlers from east of the Rocky Mountains introduced bullfrogs to California. The bullfrogs eat the smaller, native, lowland leopard frogs. Now King Stork has showed up to eat the bullfrogs! Wood storks eat fish and large insects too.

Birders come to the Sonny Bono preserve hoping to see the elusive Yuma clapper rail. Rails are marsh birds—one is hiding in the tules.

The Meadowlark and Her Children

An 1895 Rumely steam traction engine from the Antique Farm Equipment Museum in Tulare's International Agri-Center inspired this illustration. It burned wood or coal and produced ten horsepower—not even as much as most riding lawnmowers today. In those days, choice wheat-growing land was found around Stockton, and that's where this fable takes place.

The bright yellow breast of the western meadowlark is distinctively marked with a bold black "V." The meadowlark's familiar song is bubbly and cheery—an unforgettable sound of the pastures and fields.

A pocket gopher has popped up in a risky place. It will duck back into its burrow for safety.

The Lion and the Mouse

Are there really lions in California? Yes—but maybe not the kind you are thinking of, unless you are thinking of the mountain lion. "Cougar," "puma," and "catamount" are different names for the same powerful beast. Would a mountain lion really eat a little deer mouse? Yes—but it prefers bigger game, like deer, coyotes, beavers, raccoons, and hares. Watch out, mountain creatures! Nighttime is when the mountain lion—and the deer mouse—hunt for food.

Deer Mouse really knows how to stuff its face. It packs its outside cheek pouches with seeds.

Modern traps for mountain lions are like big cages with a door that drops shut. A lion in a cage is a sorry sight. It can't back up or turn around. Lion was lucky to have a smart little mouse friend to wiggle through the wire screen to help.

The "big, egg-shaped" rocks described in the fable really look that way. You can see them yourself if you visit the Alabama Hills, on the east side of the Sierra Nevada near Lone Pine. Or you can see the rocks in the movies—lots of cowboy films were made there.

A hoary bat is hard to see in the night sky. "Hoary" means grayish white, like the fur on the hoary bat's back.

The Roosters and the Eagle

Hundreds and even thousands of years ago, domestic animals like roosters, donkeys, and cows were a familiar part of everyday life. Nowadays we all know roosters go "cock-a-doodle-do," but we might need to be reminded that roosters naturally fight for the position of top bird, and even the hens have a pecking order.

It is high noon in the illustration, and Gold Wing and White Wing look like two gunfighters facing off for a showdown. On the roof, a lark sparrow waits for the barnyard battle to begin. Do you see how the roosters spread their neck feathers and wings to look bigger and tougher? Like cowboys, roosters also have spurs. Roosters can use their naturally pointed spurs for defending the hens or for fighting other males. The red things on the roosters' heads are the comb (on top) and the wattles (under the chin). They are used for cooling, because chickens don't sweat. Roosters and hens both have combs and wattles.

A sharp-eyed observer can see a golden eagle in almost any part of California. This eagle is soaring past Lassen Peak, a volcanic dome in the northern part of the state. It last erupted about one hundred years ago.

The Oak and the Reeds

Along the Kings River in central California, valley oaks grow alongside tules and cattails. The valley oaks are icons of the central San Joaquin Valley, and their distinctive long, pointed acorns provided a staple food to the region's native peoples. It was a lot of work to gather, dry, pound, and prepare the acorns to make mush. The ground squirrel and a scrub jay are collecting acorns too.

Just as iconic are the tules (or bulrushes), a kind of giant sedge. They grow from three to over ten feet tall. Native people once used them—and sometimes still do—to make skirts, boats, and mats. The heads of the cattails, a different plant, are packed with downy white fluff that seems to give personality to the two cattails illustrated here.

Have you noticed that sometimes trees look like they have faces? Oak Tree has a lumpy nose and bristly eyebrows. Also, twigs can look like fingers, and roots can look like toes. Do you think that the western fence lizard is tickling some tree toes?

The Little Crab and His Grandmother

This watery scene was inspired by visits to Point Lobos and Pebble Beach, on the central coast. Little Crab is a lined shore crab—notice the vivid green lines on his shell. Limpets, red thatched barnacles, and a chiton stick to his rock, along with droopy sea lettuce and rockweeds.

Grandmother is a spidery-looking decorator crab. She covers herself with sponges, bits of pinkish coralline algae, and flowery-looking hydroids that she sticks to tiny hooks (like Velcro) on her back.

The big rock behind her is covered here and there with barnacles, and nearby is a curtain of green surfgrass. Underwater, purple sea urchins eat algae and kelp, and the ochre star feeds on the nearby gooseneck barnacles and mussels. The big green sea anemone might look like a flower, but it is an animal, not a plant. The name "sea slug" sounds ugly, but don't you think the one in the picture, called an "opalescent nudibranch," is beautiful, with its fiery orange gills and neon blue body? Sea slugs eat anemones, barnacles, sponges, and jellyfish. Living in a tide pool sounds dangerous!

What kind of animal finds an empty seashell and moves in? That's right, the hermit crab. Can you find the hermit crab crawling away in the shell of a black turban snail?

The Prospectors and the Bear

This berry bush could be anywhere in the gold country along the Sierra Nevada—prospectors like Red Vest and Top Hat searched every stream and hillside for gold. The prospectors often came from cities in the East, expecting to find gold everywhere, and they were unprepared for the rugged country and wild animals of California.

Is it surprising that a thousand-pound bear would stop to eat berries? Grizzlies will eat all kinds of things—including mushrooms, honey, rodents, fish, or even a mule deer. Blackberry bushes are dangerous places to be if bears are around. The bushes can grow tall and can easily hide a bear.

In his 1900 book *True Bear Stories*, frontiersman Joaquin Miller recounted a story similar to this one. Miller told of an "old Indian" hunting manzanita berries who was trapped in a hollow log by a grizzly. The bear touched his nose to the head of the terrified Indian but then "shuffled on." Grizzly bears still live in Alaska and Canada but are no longer seen in California—except on the state flag!

What animal has a tail with black and white rings and lives in the forest? You will have your answer when you find the ringtail. Miners used ringtails in the mines to catch rats, which is how these creatures earned the nickname "miner's cat."

The Heron and the Fish

This story is set somewhere on the banks of Coyote Creek, which begins on the flanks of the Diablo Range, passes through San Jose, and flows into the southern end of San Francisco Bay.

Though it is known as a "green heron," greenish blue isn't the only color on the bird illustrated here: her legs and eyes are yellow; her neck is chestnut-colored; her breast is white streaked with brown; and her wing markings look like a lacy white web. With all these colors, a green heron can blend into the background and hold so very still that you do not see it, even if it is right in front of you—until it suddenly grabs at a fish.

In the fable, Heron ignores the parade of native fish, always hoping she will find something better. First to appear along the creek is a now-extinct sooty crayfish. Next in line is the three-spined stickleback, then a tule perch, and last, a steelhead trout fingerling. Steelhead are the oceangoing version of rainbow trout. It's easy to guess that a fingerling is the size of a finger. Later the trout will head for the sea and grow to weigh eight to eleven pounds or even more.

Can you find the slimy snail that Heron had to eat?

The City Mouse and the Country Mouse

Country Mouse is a brush mouse. He lives in a little burrow in the Santa Monica Mountains, just under the big sign that used to say "Hollywoodland." He is a skilled climber and likes high places. Country Mouse is a polite host and offers the first bite of a darkling beetle to his friend. These beetles can stand on their heads and squirt out a stinky fluid, so sometimes they are called "stink bugs" or "clown beetles." If Country Mouse is smart, he will stick the beetle's bottom in the dirt before eating it!

City Mouse is a house mouse—an everyday little mouse like the ones that many of you have seen. He lives in a Hollywood bungalow. Someone had a birthday party there and left all sorts of food behind. But it seems that city people have cats indoors. If the two mice could see the black house cat, they wouldn't stay to eat the snacks! You have probably seen the cat by now—if not, look for its pink tongue.

About the Author

Doug Hansen was born in Fresno, California, and is the eldest of six children in an artistic family. Doug has worked as a *Fresno Bee* newsroom artist, freelance illustrator, and cartoonist. He teaches illustration at his alma mater, California State University, Fresno. *Aesop in California* is the second children's book he has authored and illustrated for Heyday.